a **DOT** in the SNOW

STERLING CHILDREN'S BOOKS
New York

An Imprint of Sterling Publishing
1166 Avenue of the Americas
New York, NY 10036

First Sterling edition published in 2016.
Originally published in Great Britain in 2016 by Oxford University Press.

Text © 2016 by Corrinne Averiss
Illustrations © 2016 by Fiona Woodcock

ISBN 978-1-4549-2101-1

Distributed in Canada by Sterling Publishing Co., Inc.
c/o Canadian Manda Group, 664 Annette Street
Toronto, Ontario, Canada M6S 2C8

For information about custom editions, special sales, and premium and corporate purchases,
please contact Sterling Special Sales at 800-805-5489 or specialsales@sterlingpublishing.com.

Manufactured in China
Lot #:
2 4 6 8 10 9 7 5 3 1
07/16

www.sterlingpublishing.com

For our dot in the snow — C. A.

For Mum and Dad — F. W.

a **DOT** in the SNOW

Corrinne Averiss   Fiona Woodcock

STERLING CHILDREN'S BOOKS

New York

Miki wanted Mom to play in the snow,
not fish on the ice.

Snow was soft,
and fishing looked hard.
Miki wasn't ready to dive.

So he scampered away.

Up, up, up the snowy ridge.

And that's when he saw it . . .
a dot in the snow.

He raced to get a closer look.

The Dot waved its paw.

Miki sniffed.
It smelled friendly.

He liked its
twinkly face.

And the gurgling
sound it made.

Did the Dot want to play?

Yes, it did!

And then suddenly, it didn't.
A red thing was missing
from one of the Dot's paws.

Miki raced back; the ice went creak-crack!

The red thing fell into the sea. Miki dived!

The deeper it sank,
the harder he paddled.

Until he caught it!

Now the ice
was breaking everywhere.

Miki showed the Dot
how to jump.

And together they climbed,
up, up, up
to the place where they played.

But where had it gone?
Everything was white.

Everything except for . . .

A dot in the snow.

A Mommy Dot!

Two cold noses nudged goodbye.

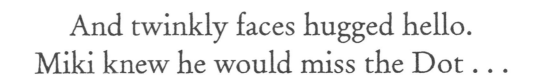

And twinkly faces hugged hello.
Miki knew he would miss the Dot . . .

But he missed his mom even more.

Paw after paw,
slow through the snow,
Miki marched back to the ice.

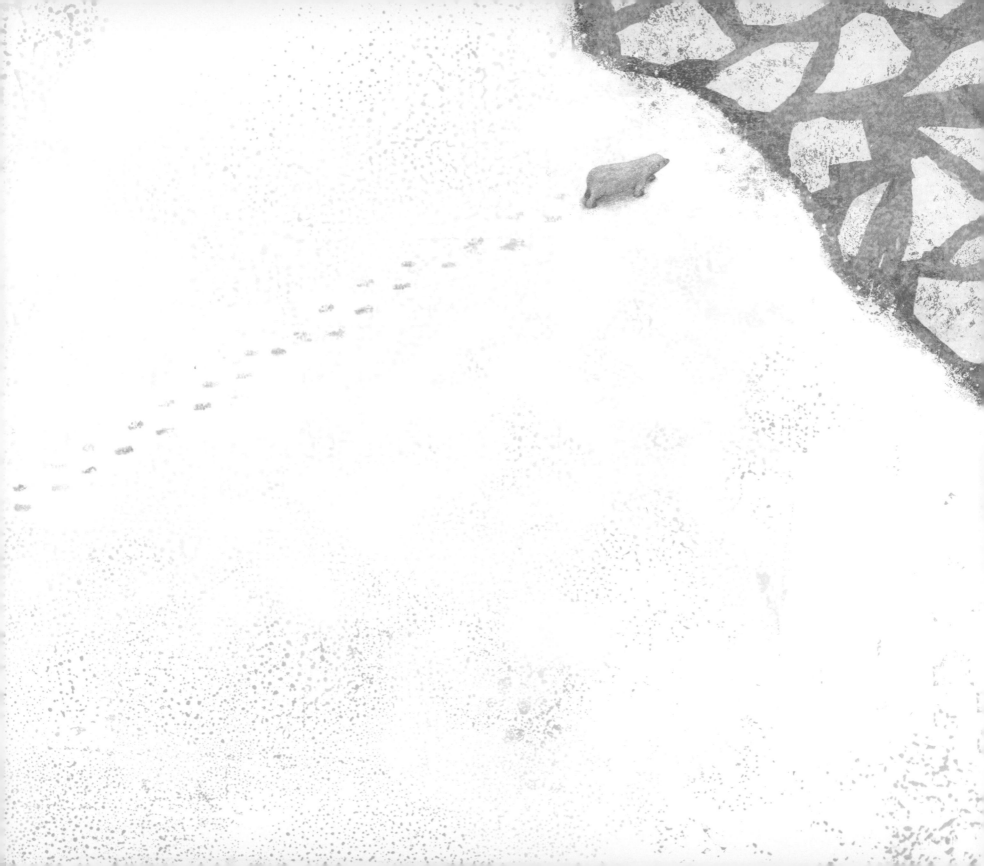

Mom, where are you?

A shape in the sea.
Could it really be . . .

Mom!

No paddling left in little legs,
Mom swam Miki to a safer spot.
He wanted to tell her all about the Dot.

But it would have to wait.
Miki dived deep,
deep into sleep.